GENE ZION

HARRY
The Dirty Dog

Illustrated by MARGARET BLOY GRAHAM

Mini Treasures

RED FOX

9 10 8

Text © 1956 Eugene Zion
Illustrations © 1956 Margaret Bloy Graham

Eugene Zion and Margaret Bloy Graham have asserted their right
under the Copyright, Designs and Patents Act, 1988
to be identified as author and illustrator of this work

First published in the United Kingdom 1956
by The Bodley Head Ltd
First published in Mini Treasures edition 1996
by Red Fox
Random House Children's Books
61-63 Uxbridge Road, London W5 5SA

Random House Australia (Pty) Limited
20 Alfred Street, Milsons Point, Sydney,
New South Wales 2061, Australia

Random House New Zealand Limited
18 Poland Road, Glenfield,
Auckland 10, New Zealand

Random House South Africa (Pty) Limited
PO Box 2263, Rosebank 2121, South Africa

Random House UK Limited Reg. No. 954009

A CIP catalogue record for this book
is available from the British Library

ISBN 978 0 099 72601 2

Printed in China

Harry was a white dog with black spots
who liked everything,
except ... having a bath.
So one day when he heard the water
running in the tub,
he took the scrubbing brush ...

and buried it in the back garden.

Then he ran away from home.

He played where they were mending the street

and got very dirty.

He played by the railway

and got even dirtier.

He played tag with other dogs

and became dirtier still.

He slid down a coal chute and got the
dirtiest of all. In fact, he changed

from a white dog with black spots,
to a black dog with white spots.

Although there were many other things to do,
Harry began to wonder if his family thought
that he had *really* run away.

He felt tired and hungry too,
so without stopping on the way
he ran back home.

When Harry got to his house,
he crawled through the fence
and sat looking at the back door.

One of the family looked out and said,
'There's a strange dog in the back garden ...
by the way, has anyone seen Harry?'

When Harry heard this, he tried very hard
to show them he was Harry. He started to
do all his old, clever tricks.

He flip-flopped

and he flop-flipped.

He rolled over and played dead.

He danced ...

and he sang.

He did these tricks over and over again
but everyone shook their heads and said,
'Oh, no, it couldn't be Harry.'

Harry gave up and walked slowly towards
the gate, but suddenly he stopped.

He ran to a corner of the garden and started to dig furiously. Soon he jumped away from the hole barking short, happy barks.

He'd found the scrubbing brush!
And carrying it in his mouth,
he ran into the house.

Up the stairs he dashed,
with the family
following close behind.

He jumped into the bathtub and sat up begging,
with the scrubbing brush in his mouth,
a trick he certainly had never done before.

'This little doggie wants a bath!'
cried the little girl, and her father said,
'Why don't you and your brother give him one?'

Harry's bath was the soapiest one he'd ever had.
It worked like magic. As soon as the children
started to scrub, they began shouting,
'Mummy! Daddy! Look, look! Come quickly!'

'It's Harry! It's Harry! It's Harry!' they cried.
Harry wagged his tail and was very, very happy.
His family combed and brushed him lovingly, and
he became once again a white dog with black spots.

It was wonderful to be home.
After dinner, Harry fell asleep
in his favourite place, happily dreaming
of how much fun it had been getting dirty.
He slept so soundly,
he didn't even feel the scrubbing brush
he'd hidden under his pillow.